Why Do Plants Have Flowers?

PLANT PARTS

Celeste Bishop

PowerKiDS
press™

New York

Published in 2016 by The Rosen Publishing Group, Inc.
29 East 21st Street, New York, NY 10010

First Edition

Editor: Sarah Machajewski
Book Design: Mickey Harmon

Photo Credits: Cover (flower) Andrekart Photography/Shutterstock.com; cover, p. 1 (logo, frame) Perfect Vectors/Shutterstock.com; cover, pp. 1, 3–4, 7–8, 11–12, 15–16, 19–20, 23–24 (background) djgis/Shutterstock.com; pp. 5, 22 Patrick Foto/Shutterstock.com; p. 6 dookfish/Shutterstock.com; p. 9 Creative Travel Projects/Shutterstock.com; p. 10 Villiers Steyn/Shutterstock.com; p. 13 nineyoii/Shutterstock.com; p. 14 Joe Petersburger/National Geographic/Getty Images; p. 17 Serg64/Shutterstock.com; p. 18 Pairoj Sroyngern/Shutterstock.com; p. 21 photka/Shutterstock.com.

Library of Congress Cataloging-in-Publication Data

Bishop, Celeste, author.
 Why do plants have flowers? / Celeste Bishop.
    pages cm. — (Plant parts)
 Includes index.
 ISBN 978-1-5081-4213-3 (pbk.)
 ISBN 978-1-5081-4214-0 (6 pack)
 ISBN 978-1-5081-4216-4 (library binding)
 1. Flowers—Juvenile literature. 2. Pollen—Juvenile literature. 3. Seeds—Juvenile literature. I. Title.
 QK653.B57 2016
 575.6—dc23
                                  2015021396

Manufactured in the United States of America

CPSIA Compliance Information: Batch #BW16PK: For Further Information contact Rosen Publishing, New York, New York at 1-800-237-9932

Contents

Plants have many different parts. They each have a job to do.

Flowers are an important part.
They help make new plants.

Flowers have **petals**. Petals have pretty colors. They also have a strong smell.

petals

Petals keep the inside
of a flower safe.

Pollen is made inside a flower. It's a yellow dust that helps make new plants.

pollen

Pollen has to travel from one flower to another. How does this happen?

Bees and bugs carry pollen between flowers. Animals, people, and the wind carry it, too.

When pollen reaches a flower, it can start making **seeds**.

Seeds are used to grow new plants.

Flowers are very important! Without them, we wouldn't have plants.

Words to Know

petal

pollen

seed

Index

Websites

Due to the changing nature of Internet links, PowerKids Press has developed an online list of websites related to the subject of this book. This site is updated regularly. Please use this link to access the list: www.powerkidslinks.com/part/flow

24